PENGUIN BOOKS

Chess

Stefan Zweig was born in Vienna in 1881, and gained fame first as a poet and translator, and then as a biographer, short-story writer and novelist. Zweig's first works were poetry and a poetic drama, *Jeremia* (1917), which expressed his passionate antiwar feelings. With the rise of Nazism, he moved from Salzburg to London to research a book on Mary, Queen of Scots. He also visited Sigmund Freud, whom he had met already in the 1920s. In 1938 he became a British citizen, and in 1940, after a successful lecture tour in South America, he and his second wife Charlotte E. Altmann settled in Brazil. Disillusioned and isolated, Zweig committed suicide with his wife, in Petrópolis, near Rio de Janeiro on 23 February 1942.

Zweig's best-known works of fiction include *Beware of Pity* (1938) and *Chess: A Novella* (1944), as well as many historical biographies of subjects as diverse as Marie Antoinette, Erasmus, Mary Queen of Scots, Magellan and Balzac.

STEFAN ZWEIG

Chess

a novella

Translated by Anthea Bell

PENGUIN BOOKS

PENGUIN BOOKS

Published by the Penguin Group
Penguin Books Ltd, 80 Strand, London WC2R 0RL, England
Penguin Group (USA) Inc., 375 Hudson Street, New York, New York 10014, USA
Penguin Group (Canada), 90 Eglinton Avenue East, Suite 700, Toronto, Ontario, Canada M4P 2Y3
(a division of Pearson Penguin Canada Inc.)
Penguin Ireland, 25 St Stephen's Green, Dublin 2, Ireland
(a division of Penguin Books Ltd)
Penguin Group (Australia), 250 Camberwell Road, Camberwell, Victoria 3124, Australia
(a division of Pearson Australia Group Pty Ltd)
Penguin Books India Pvt Ltd, 11 Community Centre, Panchsheel Park,
New Delhi – 110 017, India
Penguin Group (NZ), 67 Apollo Drive, Rosedale, Auckland 0632, New Zealand
(a division of Pearson New Zealand Ltd)
Penguin Books (South Africa) (Pty) Ltd, 24 Sturdee Avenue, Rosebank,
Johannesburg 2196, South Africa

Penguin Books Ltd, Registered Offices: 80 Strand, London WC2R 0RL, England

www.penguin.com

First published as *Schachnovelle* in 1943
Published as a Penguin Red Classic 2006
Published as a Pocket Penguin Classic 2011
008

Copyright © Stefan Zweig, 1943
Translation copyright © Anthea Bell, 2006

The moral right of the author and translator has been asserted

Set in MT Dante
Typeset by Palimpsest Book Production Limited, Falkirk, Stirlingshire
Printed in England by Clays Ltd, St Ives plc

ISBN-13: 978-0-141-02337-3

www.greenpenguin.co.uk

Penguin Books is committed to a sustainable
future for our business, our readers and our planet.
This book is made from Forest Stewardship
Council™ certified paper.

ALWAYS LEARNING   **PEARSON**

The usual last-minute bustle of activity reigned on board the large passenger steamer that was to leave New York for Buenos Aires at midnight. Visitors who had come up from the country to see their friends off were pushing and shoving, telegraph boys with caps tilted sideways on their heads ran through the saloons calling out names, luggage and flowers were being brought aboard, inquisitive children ran up and down the steps, while the band for the deck show played imperturbably on. I was standing on the promenade deck a little way from all this turmoil, talking to an acquaintance, when two or three bright flashlights went off close to us. It seemed that some prominent person was being quickly interviewed by reporters and photographed just before the ship left. My friend glanced that way and smiled. 'Ah, you have a rare bird on board there. That's Czentovic.' And as this information obviously left me looking rather blank, he explained further. 'Mirko Czentovic, the world chess champion. He's been doing the rounds of America from the east coast to the west, playing in tournaments, and now he's off to fresh triumphs in Argentina.'

I did in fact remember the name of the young world champion, and even some of the details of his meteoric career. My friend, a more attentive reader of the newspapers than I am, was able to add a whole series of anecdotes. About a year ago, Czentovic had suddenly risen to be ranked with the most experienced masters of the art of chess, men like Alekhine, Capablanca, Tartakower, Lasker and Bogolyubov. Not since the appearance of the seven-year-old infant prodigy Rzeschewski at the New York chess tournament of 1922 had the incursion into that famous guild of a complete unknown aroused such general notice. For Czentovic's intellectual qualities by no means seemed to have marked him out for such a dazzling career. Soon the secret was leaking out that, in private life, this grandmaster of chess couldn't write a sentence in any language without making spelling mistakes, and as one of his piqued colleagues remarked with irate derision, 'his ignorance was universal in all fields'. The son of a poor South Slavonian boatman, whose tiny craft had been run down one night by a freight steamer carrying grain, the boy, then twelve, had been taken in after his father's death by the priest of his remote village out of charity, and by providing extra tuition at home the good Father did his very best to compensate for what the taciturn, stolid, broad-browed child had failed to learn at the village school.

But his efforts were in vain. Even after the written characters had been explained to him a hundred times, Mirko kept staring at them as if they were unfamiliar, and his ponderously operating brain could not grasp the simplest educational subjects. Even at the age of fourteen he still had to use his fingers to do sums, and it was an enormous effort for the adolescent boy to read a book or a newspaper. Yet Mirko could not be called reluctant or recalcitrant. He obediently did as he was told, fetched water, split firewood, worked in the fields, cleared out the kitchen, and dependably, if at an irritatingly slow pace, performed any service asked of him. But what particularly upset the good priest about the awkward boy was his total apathy. He did nothing unless he was especially requested to do it, he never asked a question, didn't play with other lads, and didn't seek occupation of his own accord without being expressly told to. As soon as Mirko had done his chores around the house, he sat stolidly in the living-room with that vacant gaze seen in sheep out at pasture, paying not the least attention to what was going on around him. While the priest, smoking his long country pipe, played his usual three games of chess in the evening with the local policeman, the fair-haired boy would sit beside them in silence, staring from under his heavy eyelids at the chequered board with apparently sleepy indifference.

One winter evening, while the two players were absorbed in their daily game, the sound of little sleigh bells approaching fast and then even faster was heard out in the village street. A farmer, his cap dusted with snow, tramped hastily in: his old mother was on her deathbed, could the priest come

3

quickly to give her Extreme Unction before she died? Without a moment's hesitation the priest followed him out. The policeman, who hadn't yet finished his glass of beer, lit another pipe to round off the evening, and was just about to pull his heavy boots on when he noticed Mirko's eyes fixed unwaveringly on the chessboard and the game they had begun.

'Well, would you like to finish it?' he joked, sure that the sleepy boy had no idea how to move a single chessman on the board correctly. The lad looked up timidly, then nodded and sat down in the priest's chair. After fourteen moves the policeman was beaten, and what was more, he had to admit that his defeat couldn't be blamed on any inadvertently careless move of his own. The second game produced the same result.

'Balaam's ass!' cried the priest in astonishment on his return, and explained to the policeman, whose knowledge of the Bible was less extensive than his own, that a similar miracle had occurred two thousand years ago, when a dumb creature suddenly spoke with the voice of wisdom. Despite the late hour, the priest could not refrain from challenging his semi-illiterate pupil to a duel. Mirko easily defeated him too. He played slowly, imperturbably, doggedly, never once raising his lowered head with its broad brow to look up from the board. But he played with undeniable confidence; over the next few days neither the policeman nor the priest managed to win a game against him. The priest, who

4

was in a better position than anyone else to assess his pupil's backwardness in other respects, was genuinely curious to see how far this strange, one-sided talent would stand up to a harder test. Having taken Mirko to the village barber to get his shaggy, straw-blond hair cut and make him reasonably presentable, he drove him in his sleigh to the small town nearby, where he knew that the café in the main square was frequented by a club of chess enthusiasts with whom, experience told him, he couldn't compete. These regulars were not a little surprised when the priest propelled the red-cheeked, fair-haired fifteen-year-old, in his sheepskin coat turned inside out and his high, heavy boots, into the coffee-house, where the boy stood awkwardly in a corner, eyes timidly down-cast, until he was called over to one of the chess tables. Mirko lost the first game because he had never seen the good priest play the Sicilian Opening. The second game, against the best player in the club, was a draw. From the third and fourth games on, he defeated them all one by one.

As exciting events very seldom happen in a small South Slavonian provincial town, the first appearance of this rustic champion was an instant sensation among the assembled notables. They unanimously agreed that the prodigy absolutely must stay in town until the next day, so that they could summon the other members of the chess club, and more particularly get in touch with that fanatical chess enthusiast, old Count Simczic, at his castle. The priest, who now regarded his pupil with an entirely new pride, but although delighted by his discovery didn't want to miss the Sunday service which it was his duty to conduct, declared himself ready to leave Mirko there to be tested further. Young Czentovic was put up in the hotel at the chess club's expense, and that evening set eyes on a water closet for the first time in his life. On Sunday afternoon the chess room was full to overflowing. Mirko, sitting perfectly still at the board for four hours on end, defeated opponent after opponent without uttering a word or even looking up. Finally a simultaneous match was suggested. It took them some time to get the untaught boy to understand that a simultaneous match meant he would be playing on his own against all comers, but as soon as Mirko grasped the idea he quickly settled to the task, went slowly from table to table in his heavy, creaking boots, and in the end won seven out of the eight games.

Now earnest consultations were held. Although this new champion did not, strictly speaking, belong to the town, local pride was all afire. Perhaps the little place, its presence on the map hardly even noticed by anyone before, could have the honour of launching a famous man into the world for the first time ever. An agent called Koller, whose usual job was simply to lay on chanteuses and female singers for the garrison's cabaret, said that if there were funds available to cover a year he was ready and willing to have the young man expertly trained in the art of chess by an excellent minor master whom he knew in Vienna. Count Simczic, who in sixty years of playing chess daily had never encountered such a remarkable opponent, immediately signed an agreement. That was the day when the astonishing career of the boatman's son took off.

Within six months Mirko had mastered all the technical mysteries of chess, although with one curious reservation, which was frequently observed and mocked in chess-playing circles later. For Czentovic never managed to play a single game of chess from memory – or blindfold, as they say in the profession. He entirely lacked the ability to draw up his battlefield in the boundless space of the imagination, and always needed to have the black and white board with its sixty-four squares and thirty-two chessmen tangibly present. Even at the height of his international fame he always travelled with a folding pocket chess set, so that if he wanted to reconstruct a championship game or solve some problem, he had the position visible before him. This defect, trifling in itself, showed a lack of imaginative power, and was discussed in the inner circles of chess as heatedly as if, in a musical context, an outstanding virtuoso or conductor had proved unable to play or conduct without a score open in front of him. However, this curious quality did not delay Mirko's stupendous rise in the least. At seventeen, he had already won a dozen chess prizes; at eighteen he was champion of Hungary, and at the age of twenty he finally captured the world championship. The most audacious of champions, every one of them immeasurably superior to him in intellectual talents, imagination and daring, fell victim to his cold, tenacious logic, just as Napoleon was defeated by the ponderous Kutuzov, or Hannibal by Fabius Cunctator, of whom Livy says that he too showed striking signs of apathy and imbecility in his childhood. So it was that the illustrious gallery of chess grandmasters, who unite in their ranks all kinds of intellectual superiority, who are philosophers, mathematicians, whose natures are calculating, imaginative and often creative, found their company invaded for the first time by a complete stranger to the world of the mind, a stolid, taciturn, rustic youth from whom even the wiliest of journalists never succeeded in coaxing a single word that was the least use for publicity purposes. It was true that what Czentovic withheld from the press in the way of polished remarks was soon amply compensated for by anecdotes about his person. For the moment he rose from the chessboard, where he was an incomparable master, Czentovic became a hopelessly grotesque and almost comic figure; despite his formal black suit, his ostentatious tie with its rather flashy pearl tie-pin, and his carefully manicured fingers, in conduct and manners he was still the dull-witted country boy who used to sweep the priest's living-room in the village. To the amusement and annoyance of his chess-playing colleagues, he clumsily and with

8

positively shameless impudence sought to make as much money as he could from his gift and his fame, displaying a petty and often even vulgar greed. He travelled from town to town, always staying in the cheapest hotels, he would play in the most pitiful of clubs if he was paid his fee, he let himself be depicted in soap advertisements, and ignoring the mockery of his rivals, who knew perfectly well that he was unable to write three sentences properly, he even gave his name to a 'philosophy of chess' that was really written for its publisher, a canny businessman, by an obscure student from Galicia. Like all such dogged characters, he had no sense of the ridiculous; since winning the world tournament he regarded himself as the most important man in the world, while the knowledge that he had defeated all these clever, intellectual men, dazzling speakers and writers in their own field, and above all the tangible fact that he earned more than they did, turned his original insecurity into a cold and usually ostentatious pride.

'But how could so rapid a rise to fame fail to turn such an empty head?' concluded my friend, who had just been telling me some of the classic instances of Czentovic's childish impudence. 'How could a country boy of twenty-one from the Banat not be infected by vanity when all of a sudden, just for pushing chessmen about a wooden board for a little while, he earns more in a week than his entire village at home earns chopping wood and slaving away for a whole year? And isn't it appallingly easy to think yourself a great man when you're not burdened by the faintest notion that men like Rembrandt, Beethoven, Dante or Napoleon ever lived? With his limited understanding, the fellow knows just one thing: he hasn't lost a single game of chess for months. So, as he has no idea that there are values in this world other than chess and money, he has every reason to feel pleased with himself.'

These comments of my friend's did not fail to arouse my lively curiosity. I have always been interested in any kind of monomaniac obsessed by a single idea, for the more a man restricts himself the closer he is, conversely, to infinity; characters like this, apparently remote from reality, are like termites using their own material to build a remarkable and unique small-scale version of the world. So I did not conceal my intention of taking a closer look at this strange specimen of an intellectually one-track mind during the twelve-day voyage to Rio.

However – 'You won't have much luck there,' my friend warned me. 'As far as I know, no one has ever yet managed to extract the faintest amount of psychological material from Czentovic. For all his severe limitations, he's a wily peasant and shrewd enough not to present himself as a target, by the simple means of avoiding all conversation except with fellow countrymen of his own background, whom he seeks out in small inns. When he feels he's in the presence of an educated person he goes into his shell, so no one can boast of ever hearing him say something stupid, or of having assessed the apparently unplumbed depths of his ignorance.'

In fact my friend turned out to be right. During the first few days of our voyage, it proved completely impossible to get close to Czentovic without being actually importunate, which is not my way. He did sometimes walk on the promenade deck, but always with his hands clasped behind his back in that attitude of proud self-absorption adopted by Napoleon in his famous portrait; in addition, he always made his peripatetic rounds of the deck so rapidly and jerkily that you would have had to pursue him at a trot if you were to speak to him. And he never showed his face in the saloons, the bar or the smoking-room. As the steward told me in confidence, he spent most of the day in his cabin, practising or going back over games of chess on a large board.

After three days I began to feel positively irked by the fact that his doggedly defensive technique was working better than my will to approach him. I had never before in my life had a chance to become personally acquainted with a chess grandmaster, and the more I tried to picture such a man's nature, the less I could imagine a form of cerebral activity revolving exclusively, for a whole lifetime, around a space consisting of sixty-four black and white squares. From my own experience, I knew the mysterious attraction of the 'royal game', the only game ever devised by mankind that rises magnificently above the tyranny of chance, awarding the palm of victory solely to the mind, or rather to a certain kind of mental gift. And are we not guilty of offensive disparagement in calling chess a game? Is it not also a science and an art, hovering between those categories as Muhammad's coffin hovered between heaven and earth, a unique link between pairs of opposites: ancient yet eternally new; mechanical in structure, yet made effective only by the imagination; limited to a geometrically fixed space, yet with unlimited combinations; constantly developing, yet sterile; thought that leads nowhere; mathematics calculating nothing; art without works of art; architecture without substance – but nonetheless shown to be more durable in its entity and existence than all books and works of art; the only game that belongs to all nations and all eras, although no one knows what god brought it down to earth to vanquish boredom, sharpen the senses and stretch the mind. Where does it begin and where does it end? Every child can learn its basic rules, every bungler can try his luck at it, yet within that immutable little square it is able to bring forth a particular species of masters who cannot be compared to anyone else, people with a gift solely designed for chess, geniuses in their specific field who unite vision, patience and technique in just the same proportions as do mathematicians, poets, musicians, but in different stratifications and combinations. In the old days of the enthusiasm for physiognomy, a physician like Gall might perhaps have dissected a chess champion's brain to find out whether some particular twist or turn in the grey matter, a kind of chess muscle or chess bump, is more developed in such chess geniuses than in the skulls of other mortals. And how intrigued such a physiognomist would have been by the case of Czentovic, where that specific genius appeared in a setting of absolute intellectual lethargy, like a single vein of gold in a hundredweight of dull stone. In principle, I had always realized that such a unique, brilliant game must create its own matadors, but how difficult and indeed impossible it is to imagine the life of an intellectually active human being whose world is reduced entirely to the narrow one-way traffic between black and white, who seeks the triumphs of his life in the mere movement to and fro, forward and back of thirty-two chessmen, someone to whom a new opening, moving knight rather than pawn, is a great deed, and his little corner of immortality is tucked away in a book about chess – a human being, an intellectual human being who constantly bends the entire force of his mind on the ridiculous task of forcing a wooden king into the corner of a wooden board, and does it without going mad!

And now, for the first time, such a phenomenon, such a strange genius, or such an enigmatic fool was physically close to me for the first time, six cabins away on the same ship, and I, unlucky man that I am, I whose curiosity about intellectual matters always degenerates into a kind of passion, was to be unable to approach him. I began thinking up the most ridiculous ruses: for instance, tickling his vanity by pretending I wanted to interview him for a major newspaper, or appealing to his greed by putting forward the idea of a profitable tournament in Scotland. But finally I reminded myself that the sportsman's tried and tested method of luring a capercaillie out is to imitate its mating cry. What could be a better way of attracting a chess champion's attention than to play chess myself?

Now I have never been a serious chess player, for the simple reason that I have always approached the game light-heartedly and purely for my own amusement. If I sit at the chessboard for an hour, I don't do it to exert myself; on the contrary, I want to relax from intellectual strain. I 'play' at chess, literally, while other, real chess players 'work' at the game. But in chess, as in love, you must have a partner, and I didn't yet know whether there were other chess enthusiasts on board besides the two of us. Hoping to lure any of them present out of hiding, I set a primitive trap in the smoking-room, by acting as a decoy and sitting at a chessboard with my wife, although she is an even weaker player than I am. And sure enough, we hadn't made six moves before someone passing by stopped, another man asked to be allowed to watch, and finally the partner I hoped for came along. His name was McConnor and he was a Scot, a civil engineer who, I heard, had made a great fortune drilling for oil in California. In appearance he was a sturdy man with pronounced, angular cheekbones, strong teeth and a high complexion, its deep red hue probably due, at least in part, to his lavish consumption of whisky. Unfortunately his strikingly broad, almost athletically energetic shoulders were evidence of his character even in a game, for this Mr McConnor was one of those men obsessed by their own success who feel that defeat, even in the least demanding of games, detracts from their self-image. Used to getting his own way without regard for others, and spoilt by his very real success, this larger-than-life, self-made man was so firmly convinced of his own superiority that he took offence at any opposition, seeing it as unseemly antagonism, almost an insult to him. When he lost the first game he was surly, and began explaining at length in dictatorial tones that it could only be the result of momentary inattention; at the end of the third, he blamed the noise in the saloon next door for his failure; he was never happy to lose a game without immediately demanding his revenge. At first this ambitious determination amused me; finally I took it as no more than the inevitable side effect of my own aim of luring the world champion to our table.

On the third day my ruse succeeded, although only in part. Whether Czentovic, looking through the porthole, had seen us at the chessboard from the promenade deck, or whether it was mere chance that he honoured the smoking-room with his presence I don't know, but at any rate, as soon as he saw us amateurs practising his art, he automatically came a step closer, and from this measured distance cast a critical glance at our board. It was McConnor's move. And that one move seemed enough to tell Czentovic how unworthy of his expert interest it would be to follow our amateurish efforts any further. With the same instinctive gesture one of my own profession might use in putting down a bad detective story offered to him in a bookshop, not even leafing through it, he walked away from our table and left the smoking-room. Weighed in the balance and found wanting, I told myself, slightly irritated by his cool, scornful glance, and to vent my annoyance somehow or other I said, turning to McConnor, 'The champion doesn't seem to have thought much of your move.'

'What champion?'

I explained that the gentleman who had just passed us and taken a disapproving look at our game was Czentovic the chess champion. Well, I added, we'd both get over it and be reconciled to his illustrious scorn without breaking our hearts; the poor must cut their coat according to their cloth. But to my surprise my casual information had a completely unexpected effect on McConnor. He immediately became excited, forgot about our game, and his ambitious heart began thudding almost audibly. He'd had no idea, he said, that Czentovic was on board. Czentovic absolutely must play him. He had never in his life played a champion, except once at a simultaneous match with forty others; even that had been extremely exciting, and he had almost won then. Did I know the champion personally? I said no. Wouldn't I speak to him and ask him to join us? I declined, on the grounds that to the best of my knowledge Czentovic wasn't very willing to make new acquaintances. Anyway, what could tempt a world champion to mingle with us third-rate players?

I shouldn't have made that remark about third-rate players to such an ambitious man as McConnor. He leaned back, displeased, and said curtly that for his part he couldn't believe Czentovic would turn down a civil invitation from a gentleman; he'd see to that. At his request I gave him a brief personal description of the chess champion, and the next moment, abandoning our chessboard, he was storming after Czentovic on the promenade deck with unrestrained impatience. Yet again, I felt there was no holding the possessor of such broad shoulders once he had thrown himself into a venture.

I waited in some suspense. After ten minutes McConnor came back, not, it seemed to me, in a very good mood.

'Well?' I asked.

'You were right,' he said, rather annoyed. 'Not a very pleasant gentleman. I introduced myself, told him who I was. He didn't even give me his hand. I tried to tell him how proud and honoured all of us on board would be if he'd play a simultaneous game against us. But he was damn stiff about it; he was sorry, he said, but he had contractual obligations to his agents, and they expressly forbade him to play without a fee when he was on tour. His minimum was two hundred and fifty dollars a game.'

I laughed. 'I'd never have thought pushing chessmen from black squares to white could be such a lucrative business. I hope you took your leave of him with equal civility.'

But McConnor remained perfectly serious. 'The game's to be tomorrow afternoon at three, here in the smoking-room. I hope we won't be so easily crushed.'

'What? Did you agree to pay him two hundred and fifty dollars?' I cried in dismay.

'Why not? *C'est son métier.* If I had toothache and there happened to be a dentist on board, I wouldn't ask him to pull my tooth out for nothing. The man's quite right to name a fat fee; the real experts in any field are good businessmen too. As far as I'm concerned, the more clear-cut a deal is the better. I'd rather pay cash than have a man like Mr Czentovic do me a favour and find myself obliged to thank him in the end. And after all, I've lost over two hundred and fifty dollars in an evening at our club before, and without playing a champion. It's no disgrace for "third-rate" players to be beaten by the likes of Czentovic.'

I was amused to see how deeply I had wounded McConnor's *amour propre* with my innocent remark about 'third-rate' players. But since he was minded to pay for this expensive bit of fun, I had no objection to his misplaced ambition, which would finally get me acquainted with that oddity

Czentovic. We made haste to inform the four or five gentlemen who had already proclaimed themselves chess players about the forthcoming event, and so as to be disturbed as little as possible by people passing by, we reserved not only our table but the one next to it for the coming match.

Next day all the members of our small group had turned up at the appointed hour. The place in the centre of the table, opposite the champion, was of course taken by McConnor, who relieved his nervousness by lighting cigar after large cigar, and glancing at the time again and again. But the world champion – as I had already thought likely from what my friend said about him – kept us waiting a good ten minutes, thus heightening the effect when he appeared. He walked over to the table with calm composure. Without introducing himself – a discourtesy which seemed to say, 'You know who I am, and I don't care who you are' – he began making the practical arrangements with dry professionalism. Since there were not enough chessboards available on the ship for a simultaneous match, he suggested that we all of us play him together. After every move he would go to another table at the far end of the room, to avoid disturbing our deliberations. As soon as we had made our move, and since unfortunately there was no little bell available on the table, we were to tap a glass with a spoon. He suggested ten minutes as the maximum time for deciding on a move, unless we preferred some other arrangement. Of course, we agreed to all his suggestions like shy school-boys. The draw for colours gave Czentovic Black; he made his first move still standing there, and immediately moved away to wait in the place he had chosen, where he leaned casually back, leafing through an illustrated magazine.

There's not much point in describing the game. Of course it ended, as it was bound to end, in our total defeat as early as the twenty-fourth move. In itself, there was nothing surprising in a world chess champion's ability to sweep away half a dozen average or below-average players with one hand tied behind his back; what really depressed us all was the obvious way in which Czentovic made us feel only too clearly that it *was* with one hand tied behind his back he was defeating us. He never did more than cast an apparently fleeting glance at the board, looking past us with as little interest as if we were inanimate wooden figures ourselves, and his insolent manner instinctively reminded us of the way you might throw a mangy dog a morsel of food while turning your eyes away. With a little sensitivity, I thought, he might have pointed out our mistakes, or encouraged us with a friendly word. Even after the match, however, that inhuman chess automaton said not a word after 'Checkmate', but waited motionless at the table to see if we wanted another game with him. I had risen to my feet, helpless as one always is in the face of thick-skinned incivility, to indicate with a gesture that now this financial transaction was completed the pleasure of our acquaintance was over, at least for my part, when to my annoyance McConnor, beside me, said hoarsely, 'A rematch!'

I was quite alarmed by his challenging tone of voice; in fact, at this moment McConnor gave the impression of a boxer about to lash out rather than a gentleman in polite society. Whether it was the unpleasant nature of the treatment meted out to us by Czentovic, or just his own pathologically touchy pride, McConnor seemed a completely different man. Red in the face right up to his hair-line, nostrils flaring with internal pressure, he was visibly perspiring, and a deep line ran from his compressed lips to the belligerent thrust of his chin. In his eyes, as I saw with concern, was the light of the uncontrolled passion that usually seizes on people only at the roulette table, when they have been constantly doubling their stakes and the right colour fails to come up for the sixth or seventh time. At that moment I knew that even if it cost him his entire fortune, this fanatically ambitious man would play and play and play against Czentovic, on his own or with someone else, until he had won at least a single game. If Czentovic stayed the course he had found a gold-mine in McConnor, and could mint a few thousand dollars by the time he reached Buenos Aires.

Czentovic was unmoved. 'By all means,' he politely replied. 'You gentlemen take Black this time.'

The second game went just the same way as the first, except that several curious onlookers had made our circle not just larger but also livelier. McConnor was gazing at the board as fixedly as if he intended to magnetize the chessmen by his will to win; I sensed that he would happily have given a thousand dollars for the joy of crying 'Checkmate!' to his cold, insensitive opponent. Curiously, something of his grimly excited determination passed unconsciously to us. Every single move was discussed far more passionately than before; one of us would keep holding the others back at the last moment before we united in giving the signal that brought Czentovic back to our table. Slowly, we had reached the thirty-seventh move, and to our own astonishment were in a position that seemed surprisingly advantageous, for we had succeeded in bringing the pawn in file c to the penultimate square c_2; we had only to move it to c_1 to promote it to a new queen. We didn't in fact feel particularly comfortable about this over-obvious chance; we all suspected that the advantage we appeared to have won must have been intentionally thrown out as bait by Czentovic, whose view of the situation ranged far wider. But despite intensive study and discussion among ourselves, we couldn't see the concealed trick. Finally, as the agreed deadline approached, we decided to risk the move. McConnor had already put out his hand to the pawn to move it to the last square when he felt his arm abruptly taken, while someone whispered quietly and urgently, 'For God's sake, no!'

We all instinctively turned. A man of about

forty-five, whose thin, angular face I had already noticed on the promenade deck because of its strange, almost chalky pallor, must have joined us in the last few minutes as we were lending our entire attention to the problem. He quickly added, feeling our eyes on him, 'If you make a queen now, he'll take her at once with the bishop on c1, and you'll counter with the knight. But meanwhile he'll take his passed pawn to d7, endangering your rook, and even if you check him with the knight, you'll lose after nine or ten moves. It's almost the same combination as Alekhine used against Bogolyubov at the grand tournament in Pistyan in 1922.'

The surprised McConnor withdrew his hand from the piece, and stared in no less amazement than the rest of us at the man who had unexpectedly come to our aid like an angel from heaven. Someone who could work out a checkmate nine moves ahead must be an expert of the first rank, perhaps even a rival for the championship travelling to the same tournament, and his sudden arrival and intervention at this critical moment had something almost supernatural about it. McConnor was the first to pull himself together.

'What would you advise?' he whispered in agitation.

'I wouldn't advance just yet, I'd take evasive action first! Above all, move the king out of danger from g8 to h7. That will probably make him attack the other flank, but you can parry the attack with rook c8 to c4; it will cost him two tempos, a pawn, and his advantage. Then it's passed pawn against passed pawn, and if you defend properly you can draw with him. You can't get anything better.'

Yet again we were astonished. There was something bewildering about his precision as well as the speed of his calculations; it was as if he were reading the moves from the pages of a book. But anyway, the unexpected prospect of drawing our game against a grandmaster thanks to his intervention was enchanting. We all moved aside to give him a clear view of the board. McConnor asked again, 'King g8 to h7, then?'

'Yes, yes! Evasive action, that's the thing!'

McConnor complied, and we tapped the glass. Czentovic returned to our table with his usual regular tread, and took in the counter-move at a single glance. Then he moved the pawn from h2 to h4 on the king's flank, just as our unknown helper had predicted. The man was already whispering urgently:

'Rook forward, rook forward, c8 to c4, then he'll have to cover his pawn first. But that won't help him! Ignore his passed pawn, move your knight d3 to e5, and the balance will be restored. Keep the pressure on, advance instead of defending!'

We didn't understand what he meant. As far as we were concerned he might have been speaking Chinese. But once under his spell McConnor moved as he advised without stopping to think about it. We tapped the glass again to call Czentovic back. For the first time he did not decide on his next move at once, but looked at the board intently. Involuntarily, he drew his brows together. Then he made exactly the move that the stranger had predicted, and turned to walk away. But before he did so, something new and unexpected happened. Czentovic looked up and studied our ranks; he obviously wanted to find out who was putting up such energetic resistance all of a sudden.

From that moment on our excitement knew no bounds. Up till this moment we had played without any serious hope, but now the idea of breaking through Czentovic's cold pride sent fire flying through all our veins. And our new friend had already told us the next move, so we were able – my fingers shook as I tapped the glass with the spoon – to call Czentovic back. Now came our first triumph. Czentovic, who until this point had made his moves standing, hesitated – hesitated and finally sat down. He sat slowly and ponderously, but from the purely physical viewpoint the action cancelled out his condescending attitude towards us so far. We had forced him to come down to our level, at least in spatial terms. He thought for a long time, eyes lowered and intent on the board, so that you could hardly see his pupils under his dark lids, and in his meditations his mouth gradually dropped open, giving his round face a rather simple expression. Czentovic thought for several minutes, then made his move and stood up. And our friend was already whispering:

'Delaying tactics! Good thinking! But don't fall

for it! Force an exchange, you must force an exchange, and then we can get a draw and no god will be able to help him.'

McConnor did as he said. In the next few moves between the two of them – the rest of us had long since sunk to the status of mere extras – a back-and-forth procedure that meant nothing at all to us ensued. After about seven moves Czentovic thought for some time, then looked up and said, 'Game drawn.'

For a moment there was total silence. We suddenly heard the sound of the waves and the jazz music playing in the saloon, we could hear every step on the promenade deck and the quiet, soft blowing of the wind as it came through the cracks around the portholes. We were hardly breathing; it had happened too suddenly, and all of us were left in shock by the improbable way in which this unknown had forced his will on the world champion, in a game that was half lost already. McConnor leaned back with a sudden movement, the breath he had been holding emerged audibly from his lips in a contented 'Ah!' Myself, I was watching Czentovic. It seemed to me that during the last few moves he had turned paler. But he was good at keeping control over himself. He persisted in his apparently unruffled composure, and just asked in the most casual of tones, sweeping the chessmen off the board with a steady hand, 'Would you gentlemen care for a third game?'

He asked the question purely objectively, purely

as a matter of business. But the remarkable thing was that he had not been looking at McConnor, and instead had raised his eyes to gaze keenly straight at our saviour. Just as a horse recognizes a new and better rider by his firmer seat, he must have identified his true, genuine opponent during those last moves. Instinctively, we followed the direction of his eyes, and looked at the stranger in suspense. However, before he could think about it, let alone answer, McConnor in his ambitious excitement was triumphantly calling out to him, 'Of course! But now you must play against him on your own! You against Czentovic!'

Here, however, something unforeseen happened. The stranger, who curiously enough was still staring hard at the now empty chessboard, started when he felt that all eyes were turned on him and heard us appealing to him so enthusiastically. His expression became confused.

'Oh, by no means, gentlemen,' he stammered in visible dismay. 'Quite out of the question . . . you mustn't think of me for a moment . . . I haven't sat at a chessboard for twenty, no, twenty-five years . . . and only now do I see how improperly I behaved, interfering in your game without asking . . . please excuse my presumption.' And before we had recovered from our surprise, he had already turned and left the saloon.

'But that's impossible!' thundered the tempera-mental McConnor, slamming his fist on the table. 'The man says he hasn't played chess for twenty-five years? Out of the question! He calculated every move, every counter-attack for five or six moves in advance. No one can do that off the cuff. It's absolutely impossible – isn't it?'

With this last question McConnor had instinctively turned to Czentovic. But the world champion remained as cool as ever.

'I really can't venture an opinion. Anyway, the gentleman played in a rather strange and interesting way, so I gave him a chance on purpose.' Rising casually to his feet as he spoke, he added in his matter-of-fact manner, 'If he, or indeed you gentlemen, would care for another game tomorrow, I'm at your disposal from three in the afternoon.'

We couldn't suppress a slight smile. All of us knew that Czentovic had definitely not been generous enough to give our unknown helper a chance, and his remark was nothing but a naive excuse to mask his own failure. Our wish to see such unswerving arrogance taken down a peg or two grew all the stronger. Suddenly we peaceable, easy-going passengers were overcome by a wild, overweening lust for battle. The idea that here on this ship, in the middle of the ocean, the palm of victory might be snatched from the chess champion – a record that would be flashed all over the world by telegraph offices – fascinated us in the most provocative way. And then there was the intriguing mystery arising from our saviour's unexpected intervention just at the critical moment, and the contrast between his almost timorous modesty and the professional's unshakeable self-confidence. Who was this stranger? Had chance brought a hitherto undiscovered chess genius to light here? Or was a famous master concealing his name from us for some unknown reason? We discussed all these possibilities with great excitement; even the most audacious hypotheses did not seem to us audacious enough to reconcile the stranger's baffling shyness and surprising protestations with his unmistakable skill. On one point, however, we were all agreed; we weren't giving up the spectacular prospect of another encounter. We decided to try every possible means of persuading our helper to play a game against Czentovic the next day. McConnor pledged himself to meet the expense. Since inquiries put to the steward had by now produced the information that the unknown man was an Austrian, I was charged, as his fellow countryman, to convey our request to him.

It didn't take me long to track down the man who had fled in such haste. He was on the promenade deck, reclining in his deckchair and reading. Before going closer, I took the opportunity of observing him. His head with its sharply cut features was resting on the cushion in a slightly weary attitude; once again I was particularly struck by the strange pallor of his relatively young face, framed at the temples by dazzlingly white hair. I don't know why, but I had a feeling that this man must have aged very suddenly. I had hardly approached him before he rose courteously, and introduced himself by a name that was immediately familiar to me as that of a highly regarded old Austrian family. I remembered that a man of the same name had belonged to the circle of Schubert's most intimate friends, and one of the old Emperor's physicians had been a family member too. When I put our request to Dr B., asking him to accept Czentovic's challenge, he was obviously taken aback. It turned out that he had never guessed he had acquitted himself so well in our game against a grandmaster, indeed the most successful grandmaster of all at the time. For some reason the information seemed to make a particular impression on him, for he kept asking again and again whether I was sure that his opponent had really been the acknowledged world champion. I soon realized that this fact made my errand easier, and I merely thought it advisable, sensing the delicacy of his feelings, not to tell him that the financial risk of possible defeat would be covered by McConnor's funds. After considerable hesitation, Dr B. said he was prepared to play a game, but he expressly asked me to warn the other gentlemen not on any account to expect too much of his skill.

'For,' he added, with the smile of a man lost in thought, 'I really don't know if I'm capable of playing a game of chess properly by all the rules. Do please believe me, it wasn't false modesty when I said that I haven't touched a chessman since my schooldays, more than twenty years ago. And even then I was considered only a player of no special talent.'

He said this in such a natural way that I could not for a moment doubt his honesty. Yet I couldn't help expressing my surprise at the precision with which he could remember every single combination thought up by many different masters; he must at least, I said, have taken a great theoretical interest in the game. Dr B. smiled again in that curiously dreamy way.

'A great theoretical interest? God knows, I can certainly say I've done that. But it was under very special, indeed unprecedented circumstances. It's a rather complicated story, but it could make some slight contribution to the history of these delightful times of ours. If you have half an hour to spare . . .'

He had indicated the deckchair next to his, and I was happy to accept his invitation. We had no neighbours. Dr B. took off his reading glasses, put them aside, and began:

'You were kind enough to say that, as a Viennese yourself, you remembered the name of my family. But I don't suppose you will have heard of the legal practice that I ran with my father and later on my own, since we didn't deal with the kinds of cases that attracted newspaper publicity, and we avoided taking new clients on principle. In fact we didn't really have an ordinary legal practice any more, we confined ourselves entirely to giving legal advice to the great monasteries and in particular administering their property. As a former parliamentary deputy of the Clerical Party, my father was close to them. In addition – and now that the monarchy is past history, I suppose this can be mentioned – management of the funds of several members of the imperial family was entrusted to us. These links with the court and the clergy – my uncle was the Emperor's physician, another of the family was Abbot of Seitenstetten – went back two generations; all we had to do was maintain them, and this inherited trust involved us in a quiet, I might even say silent form of activity, not really calling for much more than the strictest discretion and reliability, two qualities that my late father possessed to a very high degree. Through his circumspection, he succeeded in preserving considerable assets for his clients both in the inflationary years and at the time of the coup. When Hitler came to the helm in Germany and began raiding the assets of the Church and the monasteries, many negotiations and transactions on the German side of the border also passed through our hands. They were designed to save movable property at least from confiscation, and we both knew more about certain political dealings by the Curia and the imperial house than the public will ever hear about. But the inconspicuous nature of our legal office – we didn't even have a brass plate outside the door – as well as our caution, for we both carefully avoided all monarchist circles, were in themselves the best protection against investigation from the wrong quarters. In all those years, in fact, none of the authorities in Austria ever suspected that the secret couriers of the imperial house always collected and handed in their most important correspondence at our modest fourth-floor premises.

'But the National Socialists, long before arming their forces against the world, had begun to muster another equally dangerous and well-trained army in all the countries bordering on their territory: the legion of the underprivileged, of people who had been passed over or who bore a grudge. They had their so-called "cells" in every office and every business company, their spies and listening-posts were everywhere, all the way to the private offices of Dollfuss and Schuschnigg. And they had their man, as unfortunately I discovered only too late, even in our own modest legal practice. He was no more than a poor, untalented clerk whom I had offered a job at a priest's request, simply to give the office the outward appearance of an ordinary firm; in reality we used him only to run innocent errands, let him answer the telephone and do the filing – that's to say, the filing of entirely harmless, unimportant paperwork. He was never allowed to open the post; I typed all important letters myself, never making copies, I took every important document home, and conducted secret discussions only in the monastery priory or my uncle's consulting rooms. Thanks to these precautions, the listening-post saw none of our important dealings, but through an unfortunate accident the vain, ambitious fellow must have noticed that we didn't trust him and that all kinds of interesting things were going on behind his back. Perhaps in my absence one of the couriers had once incautiously mentioned "His Majesty" instead of the agreed pseudonym of "Baron Fern", or perhaps the wretched man had been opening letters on the sly – at any rate, before I suspected him of anything, Munich or Berlin had instructed him to keep watch on us. Only much later, long after my arrest, did I remember how his original lacklustre approach to his work had turned to sudden eagerness in the last few months, and he had several times almost importunately offered to take my letters to the post. So I can't absolve myself of a certain incautiousness, but after all, weren't the best of diplomats and military men taken in by Hitler's insidious tricks? The close, indeed loving attention the Gestapo had been paying me over a long period was made evident by the fact that on the very evening when Schuschnigg announced his resignation, I had already been arrested by SS men. Luckily I had managed to burn the most important of our papers as soon as I heard Schuschnigg's resignation speech on the radio, and as for the remaining documents, with the indispensable certificates for the foreign investments of the monasteries and two archdukes, I sent them to my uncle, hidden in a laundry basket and taken away by my trustworthy old housekeeper literally at the last minute, just before my door was broken down.'

Dr B. stopped to light a cigar. In the flickering light I saw a nervous tic at the right-hand corner of his mouth which I had noticed before, and which recurred every few minutes. It was only a fleeting movement, not much more than the ghost of one, but it gave a curious look of unrest to his entire face.

'You probably think I'm going to tell you about the concentration camps where everyone who kept faith with our old Austria was taken, about the humiliations, torments and tortures that I suffered there. But nothing of that nature happened. I was in a different category. I wasn't herded together with those poor souls who suffered physical and mental degradation as resentments long nurtured were vented on them, I was put into that other, very small group from which the Nazis hoped to extract either money or important information. In itself, of course my modest person was of no interest to the Gestapo. But they must have discovered that we had been the front men, administrators and intimates of their bitterest enemy, and what they hoped to get out of me was incriminating material: material to be used against the monasteries which they wanted to prove had been sequestrating property, evidence against the imperial family and all in Austria who sacrificed themselves in support of the monarchy. They suspected – and to be honest, not incorrectly – that considerable amounts of the funds which had passed through our hands were still hidden away safe from their rapacity, so they brought me in at the earliest opportunity to force these secrets out of me, using their tried and trusted methods.

People in my category, from whom important evidence or money was to be extracted, were not sent to concentration camps but kept for special processing. You may remember that our chancellor and Baron Rothschild, from whose family they hoped to extort millions, were not put behind barbed wire in a prison camp, but had what looked like preferential treatment and were taken to a hotel, the Hotel Metropole, which was also the Gestapo headquarters and where each had a room of his own. Insignificant as I was, I received the same mark of distinction.

'A room of your own in a hotel – it sounds very humane, doesn't it? However, you may believe me if I tell you that when we "prominent people" were not crammed into an icy hut twenty at a time, but accommodated in reasonably well-heated private hotel rooms, they had in store for us a method which was not at all more humane, just more sophisticated. For the pressure they intended to exert, to get the "material" they needed out of us, was to operate more subtly than through crude violence and physical torture: the method was the most exquisitely refined isolation. Nothing was done to us – we were simply placed in a complete void, and everyone knows that nothing on earth exerts such pressure on the human soul as a void. Solitary confinement in a complete vacuum, a room hermetically cut off from the outside world, was intended to create pressure not from without, through violence and the cold, but from within, and to open our lips in the end. At first sight the room I was given didn't seem at all uncomfortable. It had a door, a bed, an armchair, a washbasin, a barred window. But the door was locked day and night; no book, newspaper, sheet of paper or pencil might lie on the table; the window looked out on a firewall; a complete void had been constructed around my self and even my own body. Everything had been taken from me: my watch, so that I wouldn't know the time; my pencil, so that I couldn't write anything; my penknife, to prevent me from opening my veins; even the smallest narcotic such as a cigarette was denied me. Apart from the jailer, who spoke not a word and wouldn't answer any questions, I never saw a human face and I never heard a human voice. In that place your eyes, ears and all the other senses had not the slightest nourishment from morning to night and from night to morning. You were left irredeemably alone with yourself, your body, and the four or five silent objects, table, bed, window, washbasin; you lived like a diver under a glass dome in the black ocean of this silence, and even worse, like a diver who already guesses that the cable connecting him to the world outside has broken and he will never be pulled up from those soundless depths. There was nothing to do, nothing to hear, nothing to see, you were surrounded everywhere, all the time, by the void, that entirely spaceless, time-less vacuum. You walked up and down, and your thoughts went up and down with you, up and down, again and again. But even thoughts, insubstantial as they may seem, need something to fix on, or they begin to rotate and circle aimlessly around themselves; they can't tolerate a vacuum either. You kept waiting for something from morning to evening, and nothing happened. You waited again, and yet again. Nothing happened. You waited, waited, waited, you thought, you thought, you thought until your head was aching. Nothing happened. You were left alone. Alone. Alone.

'I lived like this for two weeks, outside time, outside the world. If a war had broken out during that time I wouldn't have heard about it, for my world consisted only of table, door, bed, washbasin, chair, window and wall, and I kept staring at the same wallpaper on the same wall; I stared at it so often that every line of its zigzag pattern has etched itself on the innermost folds of my brain as if with an engraver's burin. Then, at last, the interrogations began. You were suddenly summoned, without really knowing whether it was day or night. You were fetched and led along a few corridors to you didn't know where; then you waited somewhere, again you didn't know where, and suddenly you were standing in front of a table with a few men in uniform sitting round it. A pile of papers lay on the table: files, containing you didn't know what, and then the questions began, real and false, obvious and deceptive, cover-up questions and trick questions, and while you replied strange, malicious fingers leafed through the papers containing you didn't know what, and strange, malicious fingers wrote something in the record of the interrogation, and you didn't know what they were writing. But the most terrible part of these interrogations, for me, was that I could never guess or work out how much the Gestapo really knew about what went on in my legal office, and what they wanted to worm out of me. As I've told you, I had sent the really incriminating papers to my uncle at the last minute by way of my housekeeper. But had he received them? Had he failed to receive them? And how much had that clerk given away? How many letters had been intercepted, how many might they have extracted by now from some naive cleric in the German monasteries that we represented? And they asked questions and yet more questions. What securities had I bought for such-and-such a monastery, which banks did I correspond with, did I or did I not know a Herr So-and-so, had I received letters from Switzerland and Steenookerzeel? And as I could never guess how much they had found out already, every answer became the heaviest of responsibilities. If I let slip something they hadn't known, I might be unnecessarily delivering someone up to the knife. If I denied too much, I was doing myself no good.

'But the interrogation wasn't the worst of it. The worst was coming back to my void after the questioning, back to the same room with the same table, the same bed, the same washbasin, the same wallpaper. For as soon as I was alone with myself I tried reconstructing what I ought to have said in reply, and what I must say next time to divert any suspicion that some unconsidered remark of mine might have aroused. I thought it all over, I went back over everything, examined my own statements, checked every word of what I had said to the chief interrogator, I recapitulated every question they had asked, every answer I had given, I tried to think what they might have put down in the written record, but I realized I could never work it out, I would never know. However, once these thoughts had started up in the vacuum they wouldn't stop going round and round in my head, again and again, in ever-changing combinations, and they went on until I fell asleep. After every interrogation by the Gestapo my own thoughts took over the torment of questioning, probing and torturing me just as mercilessly, perhaps even more cruelly, for every interrogation ended after an hour, and thanks to the insidious torture of solitary confinement those thoughts never stopped. And around me, always, I had only the table, the cupboard, the bed, the wallpaper, the window, no means of diversion, no book, no newspaper, no new face, no pencil for making notes, no match to play with, nothing, nothing, nothing. Only now did I realize how diabolically ingenious the hotel-room method was, how fiendishly well devised in psychological terms. In a concentration camp you might have had to cart stones until your hands bled and your frostbitten feet fell off in your shoes, you would have slept packed together with two dozen other people in the stench and the cold. But you would have seen faces, you could have stared at a field, a cart, a tree, a star, something, anything, while here you were always surrounded by the same things, always the same, always the terrible same. There was nothing here to distract me from my thoughts, my delusions, my morbid recapitulations. And that was exactly what they intended – I was to retch and retch on my own thoughts until they choked me, and in the end I had no choice but to spew them out, no choice but to tell them everything, all they were after, handing over the information and the human beings they wanted at last. I gradually felt my nerves begin to give way under the pressure of the void, and aware of the danger I stretched them to breaking point to find or invent something to divert my mind. To keep myself occupied I tried remembering and reciting anything I had ever learnt by heart, the national anthem and the playground rhymes of my childhood, the Homer I had studied at school, paragraphs of the Civil Code. Then I tried arithmetic, adding and dividing numbers at random, but my memory was unable to hold the numbers steady in the void. I couldn't concentrate on anything. The same thought kept flickering through my mind: what do they know? What did I say yesterday? What must I say next time?

'This truly unspeakable state of affairs lasted four months. Four months – it's easy to write down: just under a dozen characters! It's easy to say: four months – two syllables. Your lips can articulate such a sound in a quarter of a second: four months! But no one can describe, assess, demonstrate to himself or anyone else how long a given period lasts in a timeless, spaceless void, and you can't explain to anyone how it gnaws away at you and destroys you, nothing, nothing, nothing around you, only the same table and bed and washbasin and wallpaper, and always that silence, always the same jailer handing in food without looking at you, always the same thoughts circling around the same object in the void until you go mad. With alarm, I realized that my brain was becoming confused. At first I had been inwardly clear during the interrogations, I had answered calmly and carefully; my ability to think what to say and what not to say at the same time was still in working order. Now I stammered in articulating even the simplest sentences, for as I spoke I was staring, hypnotized, at the pen recording my statements on paper, as if I were trying to follow my own words. I felt my strength failing me, I felt the moment coming closer and closer when I would tell them everything to save myself, tell them what I knew and perhaps even more, when I would give away a dozen human beings and their secrets to escape that choking void, without gaining any more than a brief respite for myself. One evening I really did reach that point; when the jailer happened to bring my food at that moment of suffocation, I suddenly shouted, "Take me to be questioned! I want to tell them everything! I want to make a statement! I'll tell them where the securities are, where the money is! I'll tell them everything, everything!" Fortunately he didn't hear me. Perhaps he didn't want to hear me.

'In my hour of greatest need, something quite unexpected happened, offering me a way of escape, at least for a time. It was the end of July, a dark, overcast, rainy day. I remember that last detail clearly because the rain was drumming against the windowpanes in the corridor down which I was led to be questioned. I had to wait in the chief interrogator's anteroom. You always had to wait before every interrogation; leaving you to wait was part of the technique too. First they made you nervous with the summons, with being suddenly fetched from your cell in the middle of the night, and then, once you had adjusted to the idea of interrogation, once you had prepared your mind and will to resist, they kept you waiting, a deliberately pointless wait of an hour, two hours, three hours before the interrogation itself, to tire your body and wear your mind down. And I was kept waiting for a particularly long time that Wednesday, the 27th of July; I waited standing in the anteroom for two full hours. I remember the date so precisely for a particular reason, because in the anteroom where I had to wait – of course I wasn't allowed to sit down – in the anteroom where I had to wait on my feet for two hours there was a calendar, and I can't tell you how, in my hunger for the printed word, for something written, I stared and stared at that one number, those few words on the wall: July 27th. My brain devoured them, so to speak. And then I went on waiting, waiting, staring at the door, wondering when it would finally open, trying to think what my inquisitors might ask this time, and knowing it would be nothing like what I was preparing for. In spite of all this, however, the torment of waiting and standing was a pleasure too, and did me good, because at least this room wasn't the same as mine. It was a little larger, had two windows instead of one, and it was without the bed and without the washbasin and without the crack on the window sill that I had studied a million times. The door was painted a different colour, there was a different armchair by the wall, and on the left a filing cabinet with files and a coat-stand with hangers on which were draped three or four wet army overcoats, the coats of my torturers. So I had something new and different to look at, something different at last for my starved eyes, which clutched greedily at every detail. I observed every fold of those coats, I noticed, for instance, a drop of water dangling from one of the wet collars, and absurd as it may sound, I waited with ridiculous excitement to see if that drop would finally run down the fold of the fabric, or if it would continue to defy gravity and stay there longer – in fact I stared and stared at that drop for minutes on end as if my life depended on it. Then, when at last it had rolled down, I counted the buttons on the coats, eight on one coat, eight on another, ten on the third; then I compared their lapels; my hungry eyes touched, played with, seized upon all those silly little details with an avidity I can hardly describe. And suddenly my gaze fixed on something. I had seen that the side pocket of one of the coats was bulging slightly. I went closer, and thought that the rectangular shape of the bulge told me what was inside that pocket: a BOOK! I hadn't had a book in my hands for four months, and the mere idea of a book where I could see words printed one after another, lines, pages, leaves, a book in which I could pursue new, different, fresh thoughts to divert me, could take them into my brain, had something both intoxicating and stupefying about it. Hypnotized, my eyes stared at the small bulge made by that book inside the pocket, they gazed fierily at that one inconspicuous spot as if to burn a hole in the coat. At last I could no longer contain my greed; instinctively I moved closer. The mere prospect of being able at least to feel the book through the fabric made the nerves in my hands glow to the fingertips. Almost without knowing it, I moved closer and closer. Fortunately the jailor didn't notice what must have been my strange behaviour, or perhaps he thought it only natural that a man who had been standing upright for two hours would want to lean against the wall a little. Finally I was very close to the coat, and I had intentionally put my hands behind my back so that they could touch it unnoticed. I felt the fabric, and there really was something rectangular on the other side, something flexible and rustling slightly – a book! A book! And a thought flashed through me quick as lightning: steal the book! You might succeed, and you can hide it in your cell and then read, read, read, read again at last! No sooner had the thought entered my mind than it worked like strong poison; suddenly there was a roaring in my ears and my heart began to hammer, my hands turned cold as ice and wouldn't obey me. But after the first stupefaction I moved quietly and warily even closer to the coat, keeping my eyes on my jailer all the time, and with my hands hidden behind my back I moved the book further and further up in the pocket from the outside. And then: one snatch, one slight, careful tug, and suddenly I had the small, not very thick book in my hand. Only now did I take fright at what I had done. But there was no going back at this point. Yet where was I to put it? Behind my back, I pushed the book down under my trousers where the belt held them up, and from there gradually round to my hip, so that as I walked I could hold it in place with my hand down beside the seam of my trousers in a military stance. Now for the first test. I moved away from the coat-stand, one step, two steps, three steps. It worked. It was possible to hold the book in place as I walked if I kept my hand firmly pressed to my belt.

'Then came the interrogation. It required a greater effort from me than ever, for as I answered questions I was really concentrating all my strength not on what I was saying but on holding the book in place unnoticed. Fortunately the interrogation was a short one this time, and I got the book back to my room safe and sound – I won't bore you with all the details; once, when I was halfway down the corridor, it slipped dangerously low, and I had to simulate a bad coughing fit so that I could bend over and push it back up under my belt again. But what a moment it was when I came back to my hell, alone at last, yet not alone any longer!

'You'll probably expect me to have taken the book out at once, to have looked at it, read it. By no means! First I wanted to enjoy actually having a book in my possession, artificially drawing out the delightfully intriguing pleasure of anticipation, dreaming what kind of book the one I had stolen might ideally be: first of all, very closely printed, with many, many printed characters in it, many, many thin pages, so that it would take me longer to read it. Then I hoped it would be a work to exercise my mind, nothing shallow or light, but a book that would teach me something, a book I could learn by heart, poetry, and preferably – what a bold dream! – Goethe or Homer. But finally I could no longer contain my avid curiosity. Lying on the bed, so that if my jailer suddenly opened the door he couldn't see what I was doing, I took the book out from under my belt with shaking hands.

'The first glance was a disappointment, and even

made me feel a kind of bitter anger: the book I
had carried off at such great peril and was looking
forward to with such ardent expectation was
nothing but a chess manual, a collection of a
hundred and fifty championship matches. If I
hadn't been locked and barred in I'd have flung the
book through an open window in my first rage,
for what use was this nonsense to me, what could
I do with it? As a schoolboy, like most others, I had
sat at a chessboard now and then out of boredom.
But what good was this theoretical stuff going to
be? You can't play chess without a partner, and
certainly not without chessmen and a chessboard.
Morosely, I leafed through the pages, hoping I
might yet find something there to read, a foreword,
an introduction; but I found only the bare, square
patterns of the boards for the various games, and
under them symbols of which I could make nothing
at first: a2–a3, Nf1–g3, and so on. It all seemed to
me a kind of algebra to which I had no key. Only
gradually did I work out that the letters a, b and c
were for the horizontal rows of squares, the ranks,
and the numbers 1 to 8 for the vertical rows, the
files, and they indicated the present position of each
separate chessman; that at least gave a language to
the purely graphic patterns. Perhaps, I thought, I
could make myself a kind of chessboard in my cell
and then try to play these games; like a sign from
heaven, it struck me that my bedspread so happened
to have a design of large checks. Properly folded, it
could finally be arranged to show sixty-four squares.

So I first hid the book under my mattress, tearing out only the first page. Then I began modelling the chessmen, king, queen and so on, out of small crumbs saved from my bread, in what was of course a ridiculously imperfect way; after endless effort I was finally able to reconstruct the positions shown in the chess book on my chequered bedspread. But when I tried to play the whole game through I failed entirely at first with my ludicrous breadcrumb chessmen, half of which I had coloured darker with dust. I kept getting confused during those first few days. Five, ten, twenty times I had to begin that single game again from the beginning. But who in the world had as much useless spare time as I did, the slave of the void, and who had such an immense desire to learn and so much patience available? After six days I was already playing the game flawlessly to its end, after eight more days I didn't even need the crumbs on the bedspread to picture the positions in the chess book, and after another eight days I could do without the check bedspread too; automatically, what had at first been the abstract symbols in the book – a1, a2, c7, c8 – changed inside my head into visual, three-dimensional positions. The switch was a complete success: I had projected the chessboard and chessmen into my mind, where I could now survey the positions of the pieces on the board by means of the formulae alone, just as a mere glance at a score is enough for a trained musician to hear all the separate parts of a piece and the way they

49

sound together. After another fourteen days I was easily able to play any game in the book from memory – or blindfold, as the technical expression has it – and only now did I begin to understand what immeasurable relief my bold theft had brought me. For all at once I had an occupation – a pointless, aimless one if you like, but an occupation that annihilated the void around me. In those one hundred and fifty tournament matches, I had a wonderful weapon against the oppressive monotony of my own space and time. To keep the delight of my new occupation going, I divided every day up exactly: two games in the morning, two games in the afternoon, and then a quick recapitulation in the evening. That filled my day, which used to be as form-less as jelly; I was occupied without exhausting myself, for the wonderful advantage of the game of chess is that, by concentrating your intellectual energies into a strictly limited area, it doesn't tire the brain even with the most strenuous thinking, but instead increases its agility and vigour. Gradually, in what at first had been purely mechanical repetitions of the championship matches, an artistic, pleasurable understanding began to awaken in me. I learned to understand the subtleties of the game, the tricks and ruses of attack and defence, I grasped the technique of thinking ahead, combination, counter-attack, and soon I could recognize the personal style of every grandmaster as infallibly from his own way of playing a game as you can identify a poet's verses from only a few lines. What began as mere occupation to fill the time became enjoyment, and the figures of the great strategists of chess such as Alekhine, Lasker, Bogolyubov and Tartakower entered my solitary confinement as beloved comrades. Endless variety enlivened my silent cell every day, and the very regularity of my mental exercises restored to my mind its endangered security; I felt my brain refreshed and newly polished, so to speak, by the constant discipline of thought. It was particularly evident that I was thinking more clearly and concisely in the interrogations; I had unconsciously perfected my defence against false threats and concealed tricks at the chessboard. I no longer exposed my weaknesses under questioning now, and I even felt that the Gestapo men were beginning to regard me with a certain respect. Perhaps, since they saw everyone else collapse, they were silently wondering from what secret sources I alone drew the strength for such steadfast resistance.

'This happy time, when I was systematically replaying the hundred and fifty games in that book day after day, lasted for about two and a half to three months. Then I unexpectedly came up against a dead end. Suddenly I was facing the void again. For as soon as I had played each individual game from beginning to end twenty or thirty times, it lost the charm of novelty and surprise; its old power to excite and stimulate me was gone. What was the point in replaying games again and again when I knew them all by heart, move after move? As soon as I had played the first opening, the rest of the game jogged automatically along in my mind; there was no surprise any more, no tension, no problems. To keep myself occupied and create the sense of effort and diversion that were now essential to me, I really needed another book with other games in it. But as it was impossible for me to get one, there was only one way my mind could take in its strange, crazed course; I must invent new games instead of playing the old ones. I must try to play with myself, or rather against myself.

'I don't know how far you've ever thought about the intellectual situation in this king of games. But even the briefest reflection should be enough to show that as chess is a game of pure thought involving no element of chance, it's a logical absurdity to try playing against yourself. At heart the attraction of chess resides entirely in the development of strategies in two different brains, in the fact that Black doesn't know what manoeuvres White will perform in this war of the mind, and keeps trying to guess them and thwart them, while White himself is trying to anticipate and counter Black's secret intentions. If Black and White were one and the same person, you'd have the ridiculous state of affairs where one and the same brain simultaneously knows and doesn't know something, and when operating as White can forget entirely what it wanted and intended a minute ago when it was Black. Such dual thinking really presupposes a complete split of consciousness, an arbitrary ability to switch the function of the brain on and off again as if it were a mechanical apparatus. Wanting to play chess against yourself is a paradox, like jumping over your own shadow. Well, to be brief, in my desperation I spent months trying to achieve this absurd impossibility. However, I had no option but to pursue it, if I were not to fall victim to pure madness or see my mind waste away entirely. My dreadful situation forced me at least to try splitting myself into a Black self and a White self, to keep from being crushed by the terrible void around me.'

Dr B. leaned back in his deckchair and closed his eyes for a minute. It was as if he were trying to suppress a disturbing memory by force. Once again the strange little tic that he couldn't control appeared, this time at the left-hand corner of his mouth. Then he sat up a little straighter in his deckchair.

'Well – up to this point I hope I've explained it all reasonably intelligibly to you. But I'm afraid I'm not at all sure that I can give you as clear an idea of what happened next. For this new occupation put such extraordinary pressure on the brain that it made any kind of self-control at the same time impossible. I've already told you that in my opinion playing chess against yourself is essentially absurd, but even that absurdity might stand a minimal chance with a real chessboard in front of you, since the reality of the board does allow you to distance yourself to some extent, occupy a different material territory. In front of a real chessboard with real chessmen, you can insert pauses for thought, change from one side of the table to the other in purely physical terms, seeing the situation now through Black's eyes and now through the eyes of White. But forced as I was to project these battles against myself – or with myself, if you like – into imaginary space, I had to keep the situation on all sixty-four squares clearly in my mind, and in addition calculate not just the present state of the game but the possible subsequent moves of both partners, while also – and I know how ludicrous all this sounds – imagining four or five moves in advance for each of my selves, working them out twice or three times, no, six, eight, twelve times. In this game in the abstract space of the mind I was obliged – forgive me for my presumption in asking you to think along these deranged lines – to work out four or five moves ahead as player White, and the same as player Black, combining in advance all the situations that might arise as the game developed, and I had to do it, so to speak, with two brains, White's brain and Black's brain. But even this splitting of myself wasn't the most dangerous part of my abstruse experiment; that was the fact that in devising the games independently I suddenly lost the ground under my feet and fell into an abyss. Just playing through the tournament matches as I had in the earlier weeks, after all, was nothing but reproduction, purely the re-enactment of material provided to me, and as such it was no more of a strain than learning poems by heart or memorizing legal paragraphs. It was a limited, disciplined activity, and excellent mental exercise. My two games played in the morning and two games in the afternoon were a quota that I could achieve without becoming excited; they acted as a substitute for a normal occupation, and anyway, if I went wrong in the course of a game or wasn't sure what to do next, I could always resort to the book. That was the only reason why this activity had been such a healthy, rather soothing one for my shattered nerves, because playing out games between other people didn't involve me personally; it made no difference to me whether Black or White won, since it was really Alekhine or Bogolyubov trying to win the championship, and I myself, my mind and soul enjoyed the games only as a spectator, appreciating their changes of fortune and felicitous aspects. But as soon as I tried playing against myself I began unconsciously issuing myself with a challenge. Each of my two selves, my Black self and my White self, had to compete with the other, and each separ-ately felt an impatient ambition to triumph, to win; as my Black self I felt feverish anxiety after every move to see what my White self would do next. Each of my two selves felt triumphant when the other made a mistake, and at the same time was angry with itself for its own carelessness.

'All this seems pointless, and in fact such an artificial schizophrenia, such a split of the conscious-ness, with its admixture of dangerous excitement, would be unthinkable in a normal human being in normal circumstances. But don't forget that I had been forcibly torn from all normality, I was a captive, innocent but imprisoned, I had been subtly tormented with solitary confinement for months, I was a man who had long wished to vent his pent-up fury on something. And as I had nothing but this pointless game against myself, my fury and desire for revenge were injected, with fanatical enthusiasm, into the game itself. Something in me wanted to be proved right, and I had only that other self within me to oppose, so during the game I worked myself up into almost manic agitation. At first I had thought calmly, soberly, I had paused between one game and the next so that I could recover from the strain, but gradually my inflamed nerves wouldn't let me wait. As soon as my White self had made a move, my Black self was fever-ishly advancing; as soon as a game was over I was challenging myself to the next, because each time one of my chess selves was defeated by the other it wanted its revenge. I shall never be able to say even approximately how many games I played against myself during those last months in my cell, as a result of this insatiable derangement – perhaps a thousand, perhaps more. It was an obsession against which I had no defence; from morning to night I thought of nothing but bishops and pawns, rooks and kings, a and b and c, checkmate and castling. All my being and feeling drove me to the chequered square. My delight in playing turned to a lust for playing, my lust for playing into a compulsion to play, a mania, a frenetic fury that filled not only my waking hours but also came to invade my sleep. I could think of nothing but chess, I thought only in chess moves and chess problems; sometimes I woke with my forehead perspiring and realized that I must still have been unconsciously playing even as I slept, and when I dreamed of people I did so exclusively in terms of the movements of the bishop, the rook, the knight's leaps forward and back. Even when I was summoned for interrogation I couldn't think concisely about my responsibility any more; I have an idea that during the last interrogations I must have expressed myself with some confusion, because now and then my inquisitors looked at me strangely. But all the time they asked questions and consulted each other, I was just waiting, in my disastrous passion, to be taken back to my cell to go on with my playing, my mad playing of another game and then another and another. Every interruption disturbed me; even the quarter of an hour when the jailer was cleaning my prison cell, even the two minutes when he brought me food tormented my feverish impatience. Sometimes the bowl containing my meal still stood there untouched in the evening; I had forgotten to eat as I played chess. My only physical feeling was a terrible thirst; it must have been the fever of my constant thinking and playing. I emptied my bottle of water in two draughts, and plagued the jailer for more, yet next moment my tongue felt dry in my mouth again. At last my excitement as I played

– and I did nothing else from morning to night – rose to such a degree that I couldn't sit still for a moment; I kept pacing up and down as I thought about the games, faster and faster and faster I paced, becoming more and more heated the closer the end of the game came; my desire to win, to triumph, to defeat myself gradually became a kind of rage, and I was trembling with impatience, for one of my chess selves was always too slow for the other. One urged the other on; ridiculous as it may seem to you, when one of my selves didn't counter the other self's move quickly enough I began telling myself angrily, "Faster, faster!" or "Go on, go on!" Of course I now realize that this condition of mine was a pathological form of intellectual over-stimulation, for which I can find no name but one hitherto unknown to medicine: chess poisoning. Finally this monomaniac obsession began to attack not just my brain but my body too. I lost weight, my sleep was restless and broken, when I woke up it always cost me a great effort to force my leaden eyelids open; sometimes I felt so weak that when I picked up a glass to drink I had difficulty lifting it to my lips because my hands shook so much. But as soon as the game began a wild strength came over me; I walked up and down with my fists clenched, and sometimes, as if through a red mist, I heard my own voice crying hoarsely and venomously, "Check!" or "Mate!" to itself.

'I myself can't tell you how this terrible,

unspeakable condition came to a crisis. All I know is that I woke up one morning, and it was a different waking from usual. My body felt as if it were separate from me; I was resting softly and comfortably. A heavy, beneficial weariness such as I hadn't known for months weighed on my lids, so warm and kindly that at first I couldn't bring myself to open my eyes. I lay awake for a few minutes enjoying this heavy apathy, lying there lethargically with my senses pleasantly dulled. Suddenly I thought I heard voices behind me, live human voices speaking words, and you can't imagine my delight, because for months, for almost a year, I had heard no words but the harsh, sharp, malicious remarks made by my bench of interrogators. You're dreaming, I told myself, you're dreaming. Don't open your eyes whatever you do! Let the dream go on, or you'll see your accursed cell around you again, the chair and the washstand and the table and the wallpaper with its pattern forever the same. You're dreaming – go on with the dream!

'But curiosity got the upper hand. Slowly and cautiously, I opened my eyelids. And wonder of wonders: I was in another room, a larger, more spacious room than my hotel cell. An unbarred window let daylight in, and there was a view of trees, green trees swaying in the wind instead of my rigid firewall, the walls here gleamed smooth and white, the ceiling was white and rose high above me – it was true, I was lying in another bed, one I didn't know, and human voices were whispering quietly behind me, it really wasn't a dream. I must instinctively have given a violent start of surprise, because I heard steps approaching. A woman came up to me, moving gracefully, a woman with a white cap on her hair: a nurse. A shiver of delight ran through me; it was a year since I had set eyes on a woman. I stared at this lovely apparition, and there must have been a wild, ecstatic expression in my eyes, for as she came closer the woman said soothingly but firmly, "Calm! Keep calm!" But I merely listened to her voice – wasn't that a human being speaking? And in addition – an unimaginable miracle – speaking in a soft, warm, almost tender woman's voice. I stared avidly at her mouth, for in that year of hell I had come to think it improbable that one human being could speak kindly to another. She smiled at me – yes, she smiled, so there were still people capable of a kind smile – then put an admonishing finger to her lips and walked quietly on. But I couldn't obey her. I hadn't seen enough of the miracle yet. I tried to force myself upright in the bed to watch her go, to look at the miracle of a kindly human being as she walked away. As I tried to haul myself up by the edge of the bed, however, I found I couldn't do it. Where my right hand usually was, and my fingers and wrist, I felt something strange instead: a large, thick, white wad of fabric, obviously an extensive bandage. At first I stared uncomprehendingly at this white, thick, strange thing on my hand, and then I slowly began to grasp where I was, and wondered what had happened to me. I must have been injured, or else I'd hurt my own hand. I was in a hospital.

'At midday the doctor came, a friendly, elderly man. He knew my family name, and mentioned my uncle the imperial physician so respectfully that I immediately felt he was well-disposed to me. As we talked, he asked me all kinds of questions, particularly one that surprised me – was I a mathematician or a chemist? I said no.

'"Strange," he murmured. "In your delirium you kept crying out such strange formulae – c_3, c_4. We could none of us make anything of them."

'I asked what had happened to me. He gave a rather odd smile.

'"Nothing serious. An acute irritation of the nerves." And he added quietly, after looking cautiously around, "Not surprising, after all. You've been here since March the 13th, haven't you?"

'I nodded.

'"No wonder, then, with their methods," he murmured. "You're not the first. But don't worry."

'From the way in which he soothingly whispered this, and thanks to his kind expression, I knew I was in good hands here.

'Two days later, the kindly doctor told me frankly what had happened. The jailer had heard me shouting out loud in my cell, and at first thought someone had come in and I was quarrelling with him. But no sooner did he appear in the doorway than I had rushed at him, uttering wild cries which sounded like, "Will you make your move, you rascal, you coward?" I had tried to seize him by the throat, and finally I hit out so frantically that he had to call for help. As I was being dragged off in my rabid state, I had suddenly torn myself free, rushed to the window in the corridor and smashed the pane, cutting my hand – you can still see the deep scar here. I had spent my first few nights in hospital in a kind of brain fever, but the doctor thought my senses were perfectly clear now. "To be sure," he added quietly, "I won't say that to those gentlemen, or they'll have you back in there. Trust me, and I'll do my best."

'I have no idea what that helpful doctor told my tormentors, but at least he got what he hoped to achieve: my release. He may have said I wasn't responsible for my own actions, or perhaps by now I was of no importance to the Gestapo, for Hitler had occupied Bohemia, so as far as he was concerned that was Austria dealt with. I had only to sign an undertaking to leave our native land for ever within two weeks, and those two weeks were so full of the thousands of formalities that former cosmopolitans need in order to travel these days – military papers, police papers, tax certificates, a passport, a visa, a health certificate – that I had no time to think about the past much. It seems that mysterious powers work to regulate our brains, automatically switching off what might burden and endanger the mind, for whenever I tried to think back to my time in that cell the light in my head went out, so to speak; only many weeks later, in fact only here on this ship, have I found the courage to remember what happened to me again.

'And now you'll understand why I acted to your friends in such an unseemly and probably bewildering manner. I was walking through the smoking-room entirely by chance when I saw them sitting at the chessboard, and I was instinctively rooted to the spot by surprise and horror. For I had entirely forgotten that chess can be played with a real chessboard and real chessmen; I had forgotten that two completely different people sit opposite each other in person during the game. It actually took me a few minutes to realize that the players were basically involved in the same game that, in my desperate situation, I had tried playing against myself for months. The numbers I had used to help me in my grim mental exercises had been only a substitute for those carved chessmen, a symbol of them; my surprise when I saw that the movement of the chessmen on the board was the same as the imaginary moves I had made in my mind was, perhaps, like the surprise of an astronomer who has used complicated methods to calculate the existence of a new planet on paper, and then actually sees it as a white, bright, heavenly body in the sky. As if magnetically drawn to the board, I stared at it and saw my patterns – knight, rook, king, queen and pawns – as real figures carved from wood. To get an idea of the state of the game I first had to change them automatically back from my abstract world of figures into moving chessmen. Gradually I was overcome by curiosity to see a real game between two players. Then came the embarrassing moment when, forgetting common courtesy, I intervened in your game. But your friend's wrong move was like a pang going through my heart. It was purely instinctive when I restrained him, something done impulsively, just as you'd catch hold of a child leaning over the banisters without thinking about it. Only later did I realize how very improperly my impulse had made me behave.'

I made haste to assure Dr B. that we were all extremely glad to owe the pleasure of his acquaintance to this incident, and said that after all he had told me I would now be doubly interested to see him playing in tomorrow's improvised match. Dr B. made an uneasy movement.

'No, you really mustn't expect too much. It will be only a kind of test for me . . . a test to see if . . . if I'm even capable of playing a normal game of chess, a game on a real chessboard with actual chessmen and a living partner . . . for I doubt more and more whether those hundreds, perhaps thousands of games I played were genuine games of chess and not just a kind of dream chess, delirious chess, a game played in a fever, missing out certain stages as you do in a dream. I hope you don't really expect me to get anywhere against a chess champion – in fact the world champion. What interests and intrigues me is just a retrospective curiosity to find out whether I was really playing chess in my cell or whether it was mere delusion, if I was on the edge of the dangerous precipice at the time or already over it – that's all, nothing more.'

At that moment the gong summoning us to dinner was struck at the far end of the ship. We must have talked for almost two hours – Dr B. had told his story to me at much greater length than I have set it down here. I thanked him with all my heart and took my leave. But I had not walked all the way along the deck before he followed me to add, obviously nervous, even stammering slightly, 'And one more thing! In case I should appear uncivil later, would you tell the gentlemen in advance that I will play only one game . . . it's to be the final line drawn under an old account, a last goodbye, not a new beginning. I wouldn't want to fall into that frantic passion of chess-playing a second time. I think of it now only with horror, and moreover . . . moreover, the doctor warned me too, expressly warned me. A man who has once fallen victim to a mania is always at risk, and in a case of chess poisoning, even if you're cured, it's better not to go near a chessboard. So you'll understand . . . just this one game, as a test for myself, no more.'

We assembled in the smoking-room next day punctually at the appointed hour, three o'clock. Our party had been increased by two enthusiasts for the royal game, ship's officers who specially asked for time off their duties so that they could watch the match. Czentovic did not keep us waiting as on the previous day either, and after the usual draw for colours the remarkable match between this unknown man and the famous world champion began. I am sorry that it was played only for us amateur spectators, and any record of it is lost to the annals of the art of chess, just as Beethoven's piano improvisations are lost to music. On the following afternoons we did try to reconstruct the match from memory, but in vain; during the game itself we had probably all been paying too much rapt attention to the players rather than the course of play. For the intellectual contrast between their bearing became more and more obvious as the game went on. Czentovic, the experienced player, remained motionless as a block throughout, his eyes lowered to the chessboard with a stern, fixed gaze. In him, thought seemed to be an actual physical effort requiring the utmost concentration of all his organs. Dr B., on the other hand, was relaxed and natural in his movements. As a true dilettante in the best sense of the word, one to whom, when he plays a game, it is the game itself that brings *diletto*, joy, he was entirely relaxed, talked to us during the first few pauses, explaining points, lit himself a cigarette with a light hand, and when it was his turn just looked straight at the board for a minute. Every time he seemed to have been expecting his opponent's move in advance.

The obligatory opening moves went by quite quickly. Only at the seventh or eighth did something like a definite plan appear to emerge. Czentovic spent longer thinking between moves, from which we sensed that the real battle for the upper hand was beginning. But to be perfectly honest, the gradual development of the situation was something of a disappointment to us laymen, as it is in every real tournament game. For the more the chessmen became interlocked in a strange, intricate formation, the more impenetrable did the real state of affairs seem to us. We couldn't tell what either of the opponents intended, or which of the two really held the advantage. We just noticed individual pieces being advanced like levers to break through the enemy front, but we were unable – since with these first-class players every movement was always combined several moves in advance – to see the strategic intention in all this toing and froing. And in addition a numbing weariness gradually set in, mainly because of Czentovic's endless pauses to think, which were visibly beginning to irritate our friend too. I noticed uneasily that as the game went on he began shifting more and more restlessly in his chair, now nervously lighting cigarette after cigarette, now reaching for his pencil to note something down. Then again he ordered mineral water and hastily drank glass after glass; it was clear that he could combine a hundred times faster than Czentovic. Every time the latter, after endless deliberations, decided to move a piece forward with his ponderous hand, our friend just smiled like someone who sees something long expected happen, and he quickly riposted. With his rapidly working mind, he must have worked out all the possibilities open to his opponent in advance; the longer Czentovic's decision was delayed, therefore, the more impatient he became, and as he waited a displeased, almost hostile look hovered around his lips. But Czentovic was not to be hurried. He thought hard and silently, and paused for longer and longer intervals the fewer pieces were left on the board. At the forty-second move, after they had been playing for two and three-quarter hours, we were all sitting wearily and almost indifferently around the tournament table. One of the ship's officers had already gone off, the other had picked up a book to read, and looked up for a minute only whenever there was a change on the board. But then suddenly, at a move of Czentovic's, the unexpected happened. As soon as Dr B. saw that Czentovic was taking hold of the knight to move it forward, he crouched like a cat about to pounce. His whole body began to tremble, and no sooner had Czentovic made his move with the knight than he quickly moved his queen and said, in a loud and triumphant voice, 'There! Done it!' leaned back, crossed his arms over his chest, and looked challengingly at Czentovic. A fiery light suddenly glowed in his pupils.

We involuntarily bent over the board, trying to understand the move so triumphantly announced. At first sight there was no obvious direct threat. Our friend's remark must therefore refer to some development that we amateurs, with our limited powers of thought, could not work out yet. Czentovic was the only one among us who had not moved at the challenging statement; he sat there as imperturbably as if he had entirely failed to hear that offensive 'Done it!' Nothing happened. As we were all instinctively holding our breath, you could suddenly hear the ticking of the clock which had been put on the table for timing the moves. Three minutes passed, seven minutes, eight minutes – Czentovic did not stir, but I felt as if his thick nostrils were even further dilated by some inner exertion. Our friend seemed to find this silent waiting as intolerable as we did. Suddenly he rose to his feet and began pacing up and down the smoking-room, first slowly, then faster and faster. Everyone looked at him in some surprise, but no one with more uneasiness than I did, for it struck me that for all the vigour of his tread, his steps always measured out exactly the same amount of space; it was as if he kept coming up against an invisible cupboard in the middle of the empty floor, and it obliged him to turn. With a shudder, I realized that this pacing back and forth unconsciously reproduced the dimensions of his former cell; in the months of captivity he must have marched up and down like a caged animal in exactly the same way, he must have clasped his hands and hunched his shoulders exactly like that; he must have gone up and down that cell in precisely this manner a thousand times, with the glint of madness in his fixed yet feverish gaze. However, his powers of thought still seemed entirely intact, for from time to time he impatiently turned to the table to see if Czentovic had made up his mind yet. But the wait drew out to nine and then ten minutes. Then, at last, something none of us had expected happened. Slowly, Czentovic raised his heavy hand, which until now had been lying motionless on the table. We all waited in suspense for his decision. But Czentovic did not make a move. Instead, he slowly but with a determined gesture pushed all the pieces off the board with the back of his hand. Not until the next moment did we understand: Czentovic had resigned the game. He had capitulated so as to avoid being visibly checkmated in front of us. The improbable had happened; the world champion, the grandmaster who had won countless tournaments, had lowered his colours to an unknown, a man who hadn't touched a chessboard for twenty or twenty-five years. Our anonymous and obscure friend had beaten the greatest chess player on earth in open battle!

Without noticing it, we had risen to our feet one by one. We all felt we had to say or do something to express our delighted amazement. The one man who kept still and unmoved was Czentovic. Only after a measured pause did he raise his head and look stonily at our friend.

'Another game?' he asked.

'Of course,' replied Dr B., with an enthusiasm that I did not like, and before I could remind him of his resolve to play only a single game he sat down and began setting up the chessmen again with feverish haste. He assembled them so rapidly that a pawn twice slipped through his shaking fingers and fell to the floor; the painful discomfort I had already felt at his unnatural excitement grew to a kind of fear. For an obvious mood of elation had come over the previously calm and quiet man; the tic played around his mouth more and more often, and his body trembled as if shaken by a sudden fever.

'No!' I whispered quietly to him. 'Not now! Let that be enough for today! It's too much of a strain on you.'

'A strain! Ha!' he laughed out loud, not pleasantly. 'I could have played seventeen games in that time, instead of dawdling along! The only strain I feel is in not going to sleep playing at this pace! There! You begin!'

He had spoken these last words to Czentovic, in a vigorous, almost rough tone. Czentovic looked at him, a calm and measured look, but his fixed, stony gaze had something of a clenched fist about it now. Suddenly there was something new between the two players: a dangerous tension, a passionate hatred. They were no longer two partners wanting to try out their skill on each other in play, but enemies mutually sworn to destroy one another. Czentovic hesitated for a long time before making the first move, and I had a clear feeling that he was waiting so long on purpose. Trained tactician that he was, he had obviously found out that his slow tempo itself wearied and irritated his opponent. So it took him no less than four minutes to make the simplest, most normal of all openings by moving his king's pawn the usual two squares forward. Immediately our friend countered with his own king's pawn, but once again Czentovic paused for an endless, almost intolerable time; it was like a bright lightning strike when you wait, heart thudding, for the thunder, but the thunder doesn't roll and still doesn't roll. Czentovic did not move. He thought quietly, slowly, and I became even more certain that he was thinking slowly with malice aforethought. However, that gave me plenty of time to observe Dr B. He had just drunk his third glass of water; involuntarily, I remembered how he had told me about his raging thirst in his cell. All the signs of abnormal excitement were clearly present; I saw perspiration stand out on his brow, while the scar on his hand was redder and stood out more sharply than before. But he was still in control of himself. Only when Czentovic yet again thought endlessly about the fourth move did his composure give way, and he suddenly snapped at him, 'Come along, make your move, can't you?'

Czentovic looked up coolly. 'As far as I'm aware, we agreed on ten minutes between moves. I don't play with any shorter time span, on principle.'

Dr B. bit his lip; I saw the sole of his shoe rocking restlessly, more and more restlessly up and down on the floor under the table, and I myself was made progressively more nervous by the ominous foreboding that something beyond reason was brewing in his mind. In fact there was a second incident at the eighth move. Dr B., who had been waiting with less and less composure, could no longer restrain his tension; he moved back and forth and began unconsciously drumming his fingers on the table. Once again Czentovic raised his heavy, rustic head.

'May I ask you not to drum your fingers like that? It disturbs me. I can't play in this way.'

'Ha!' barked Dr B., laughing. 'So we see.'

Czentovic's forehead reddened. 'What do you mean by that?' he asked sharply and unpleasantly.

Dr B. laughed briefly again, maliciously. 'Nothing. Only that you are obviously very nervous.'

Czentovic said nothing, but looked down. Not until seven minutes later did he make the next move, and the game dragged on at this deadly pace. You felt as if Czentovic were turning to stone; in the end he paused each time to think for the maximum period agreed before making up his mind on a move, and from one interval to the next our friend's behaviour became ever more bizarre. It looked as if he had lost interest in the game and was thinking about something else entirely. He stopped pacing rapidly up and down, and sat motionless in his place. Staring into space with a fixed, almost mad look, he kept muttering incomprehensible remarks to himself; either he had lost himself in endless combinations or else – and this was my own suspicion – he was working out completely different games, for every time Czentovic finally made his move he had to be reminded to come back to the here and now. Then it took him several minutes to find his way around the situation again, and I began to suspect ever more strongly that he had really forgotten Czentovic and all of us long ago in a cold form of derangement that might suddenly vent itself in violence. And sure enough, at the nineteenth move the crisis came. Czentovic had hardly moved his piece before Dr B. suddenly, and without looking properly at the board, pushed his bishop three squares forward, crying so loud that we all jumped, 'Check! Your king's in check!'

We immediately looked at the board, expecting to see some exceptional move. But after a minute something that none of us expected happened. Czentovic raised his head very, very slowly, and looked – as he had never done before – from one to another of us as we sat there. He seemed to be enjoying something hugely, for gradually a satisfied and clearly derisive smile began to appear on his lips. Only after he had enjoyed this triumph of his to the full – we still didn't understand it – did he turn with mock civility to address our party.

'I'm sorry, but I see no check. Do any of you gentlemen think that my king is in check?'

We looked at the board, and then we looked in concern at Dr B. The square where Czentovic's king stood was indeed, as any child could see, shielded from the bishop by a pawn, so no check to the king was possible. We became uneasy. Could our friend, in his haste, have moved a piece the wrong way, one square too far or too near? Now Dr B. himself, alerted by our silence, was staring at the board, and began stammering heatedly, 'But the king should be on f7 . . . it's in the wrong place, quite the wrong place. You made the wrong move! Everything's wrong on this board . . . the pawn should be on g5, not g4 . . . this is a completely different game. This is . . .'

He suddenly stopped. I had taken him firmly by the arm, or rather pinched his arm so hard that even in his feverish confusion he was bound to feel my grip. He turned and stared at me like a sleepwalker.

'What . . . what do you want?'

All I said was, 'Remember!' at the same time running my finger over the scar on his hand. Instinctively, he followed my movement, and his glazed eyes stared at the blood-red line of it. Then he suddenly began to tremble, and a shudder ran through his whole body.

'For God's sake,' he whispered, his lips pale. 'Have I said or done something absurd . . . can I after all have gone . . . ?'

'No,' I whispered quietly. 'But you must break this game off at once. It's high time. Remember what the doctor told you!'

Dr B. rose abruptly. 'I do apologize for my stupid mistake,' he said, in his old, courteous voice, and he bowed to Czentovic. 'Of course what I said was pure nonsense. Naturally the game is yours.' Then he turned to us. 'I must apologize to you gentlemen too. But I did warn you in advance not expect too much of me. Forgive the awkwardness of it . . . this is the last time I ever try to play a game of chess.'

He bowed and walked off, in the same inconspicuous, mysterious way as he had first appeared. Only I knew why the man would never touch a chessboard again, while the others were left, slightly confused, with the uncertain feeling of having only just avoided something uncomfortable and dangerous. 'Damned fool!' growled the disappointed McConnor. Last of all, Czentovic rose from his chair, and cast another glance at the half-finished game.

'A pity,' he said magnanimously. 'It wasn't a bad attack at all. For an amateur, that gentleman really is uncommonly gifted.'